SCOOBY-DOO!

THAT'S SNOW GHOST

Adapted by Molly Wigand

Illustrated by Scott Neely and Thomas Phong

 A GOLDEN BOOK • NEW YORK

Published in the United States by Golden Books, an imprint of Random House Children's Books, a division of
Penguin Random House LLC, 1745 Broadway, New York, NY 10019, and in Canada by Penguin Random House Canada Limited, Toronto.
Originally published in slightly different form by Golden Books in 2001. Golden Books, A Golden Book, A Little Golden Book,
the G colophon, and the distinctive gold spine are registered trademarks of Penguin Random House LLC.
rhcbooks.com
ISBN 978-0-593-42536-7 (trade) — ISBN 978-0-593-42537-4 (ebook)
Printed in the United States of America
10 9 8 7 6 5 4 3 2

"*O*oowwwooo!"

A wolf howled as Scooby and his friends entered the ski resort where they planned to spend the weekend.

"Welcome to Wolf's End Lodge!" bellowed the innkeeper, Mr. Greenway. "We have all the comforts of home."

"Whose home?" Shaggy muttered. "Dracula's?"

Just then, a nervous visitor handed Mr. Greenway a suitcase and left.

"That was Mr. Leech . . . another guest." Mr. Greenway chuckled wickedly. "Now, be sure to lock your doors tonight. Or the Snow Ghost will get you . . . and turn you into ghosts!"

Later, as Shaggy checked the locks in his room—
"*RROOAARRR!*" A gigantic furry figure appeared
outside his window!
"*Zoinks!* The Snow Ghost!" yelled Shaggy.
The friends rushed outside and hopped onto some
snowmobiles to investigate.

"This ski trip's turning into a real *scare* trip!" said Shaggy as the
friends zoomed through the woods, following the ghost's footprints.
But at the edge of a steep cliff, the monster's footprints stopped.

Suddenly, a loud, angry growl came from the sky.

"The Snow Ghost!" said Velma.

"And he can fly!" added Fred as the ghost soared down the mountain.

The friends backtracked to the patch of trees where the ghost had disappeared.

Then Velma saw something!

"Look!" Velma cried. "More footprints—and they're covered with sawdust."

"Well," said Fred, "where there's sawdust, there's usually a sawmill."

Fred was right! Just over the next hill stood
a deserted sawmill.
"Let's split up and search this place!" he said.
"Ruh-roh," whimpered Scooby.

The gang split up. Velma, Scooby, and Shaggy tiptoed into a shadowy room. Scooby and Shaggy spotted a broken mirror and started to make funny faces in it. They soon forgot all about the Snow Ghost. And they didn't see Velma getting snatched!

"Scooby! Help!" they heard her call from another
room. Scooby ran in and saw her chained to a log
that was headed for a spinning buzz saw! Time was
running out!

"Quick! Make like a beaver!" Velma screamed.

Scooby gnawed the log in half and saved Velma just in time!

"You did it, Scooby!" she exclaimed.

That was when the Snow Ghost showed up!
Thinking fast, Scooby pushed the log with Velma
on it out the door. Then he hopped aboard!

Scooby and Velma slid down a steep log chute. But the Snow Ghost pushed a bundle of dynamite after them! Scooby used his tail as a propeller and they gained speed, zipping onto a patch of ice.

Scooby and Velma were safe. They hurried back to the sawmill and found their friends.

But the Snow Ghost caught up! Shaggy and
Scooby got away. The others started to run.

"Quick! Duck behind those logs!" Fred yelled.
"We lost him!" said Velma.

Daphne found a hollow log. "Look!" she said.
"Diamonds! And jewelry!" exclaimed Fred.
"*Hmmm* . . . ," said Velma. "I think I'm beginning
to figure out this kooky deep-freeze mystery!"

When the friends met up again, no one saw the Snow Ghost creep up behind Scooby . . . until the ghost grabbed him!

"I'll save you, Scoob!" yelled Shaggy. He bent a tree back and shot a huge snowball at the ghost.

Shaggy's snowball knocked over the Snow Ghost—and Scooby, too! They both rolled down a hill.

Thump! The giant ball of snow crashed. Heads and limbs were poking out everywhere.

"I've got a headache!" someone moaned. It was the Snow Ghost!

"Mr. Greenway!" said Daphne. The Snow Ghost was just
a furry costume!

The friends had solved the mystery! They told the sheriff that
Mr. Leech had brought stolen jewels to the lodge in a suitcase,
and Mr. Greenway had used the secret hollow logs to sneak the
jewels out. By dressing up as the Snow Ghost, Mr. Greenway
had scared people away, including guests.

"But how did he fly?" the sheriff asked.

"With transparent plastic skis!" said Velma.
"Show 'em, Scooby!"
   "*Scooby-Dooby-Doooo!*" howled Scooby.
He was ready to have some fun!